ADVANCE PRAISE FOR
BEAVER HILLS FOREVER

"*Beaver Hills Forever* is full of raunch and riot. Kerr's ability to gravitate around the embodied truths of institutional whiteness, class, settler colonization, and the Indigenous (Métis) experience in the moraine of amiskwaciy is rebellious in its desire to not pathologize or rationalize the violent backdrops of its animate setting. With his skilled hand, Kerr makes sure there is 'room for [all] in the digital economy of the Future.'"
—**JOSHUA WHITEHEAD**, author of *Jonny Appleseed*

"'Not every Métis kid / Needs a sad story,' says a character in Kerr's propulsive and deeply entertaining new work, where each bone-clean sentence holds a galaxy of stories in its marrow. Kerr is part of a vital contemporary movement that is reimagining what our literatures can be and what they can do. *Beaver Hills Forever* is a reminder that laughter and passion are as much a part of the narrative as struggle. In these pages, you'll find voices that demand to be heard, felt, and remembered."
—**CARLEIGH BAKER**, author of *Last Woman* and *Bad Endings*

BEAVER HILLS FOREVER

A MÉTIS POETIC NOVELLA

CONOR KERR

ARSENAL PULP PRESS
VANCOUVER

BEAVER HILLS FOREVER
Copyright © 2025 by Conor Kerr

All rights reserved. No part of this book may be reproduced in any part by any means—graphic, electronic, or mechanical—without the prior written permission of the publisher, except by a reviewer, who may use brief excerpts in a review, or in the case of photocopying in Canada, a licence from Access Copyright.

ARSENAL PULP PRESS
Suite 202 – 211 East Georgia St.
Vancouver, BC V6A 1Z6
Canada
arsenalpulp.com

The publisher gratefully acknowledges the support of the Canada Council for the Arts and the British Columbia Arts Council for its publishing program and the Government of Canada and the Government of British Columbia (through the Book Publishing Tax Credit Program) for its publishing activities.

Arsenal Pulp Press acknowledges the xʷməθkʷəy̓əm (Musqueam), Sḵwx̱wú7mesh (Squamish), and səlilwətaɬ (Tsleil-Waututh) Nations, custodians of the traditional, ancestral, and unceded territories where our office is located. We pay respect to their histories, traditions, and continuous living cultures and commit to accountability, respectful relations, and friendship.

Arsenal Pulp Press is committed to reducing the consumption of non-renewable resources in the making of our books wherever possible. We make every effort to use materials that support a sustainable future. This book is printed on paper made with 100 percent sustainable recycled fibre content.

This is a work of fiction. Any resemblance of characters to persons either living or deceased is purely coincidental.

Cover and text design by Jazmin Welch
Cover art by Syd Danger
Copy-edited by Catharine Chen
Proofread by JC Cham

Printed and bound in Canada

Library and Archives Canada Cataloguing in Publication:
Title: Beaver hills forever / Conor Kerr.
Names: Kerr, Conor, author.
Identifiers: Canadiana (print) 20250141981 | Canadiana (ebook) 20250153114 |
    ISBN 9781834050089 (softcover) | ISBN 9781834050096 (EPUB)
Subjects: LCGFT: Novels in verse.
Classification: LCC PS8621.E7636 B43 2025 | DDC C811/.6—dc23

FOR EDMONTON

CONTENTS

PART ONE:
MOOSE MEAT

09

PART TWO:
PRAIRIE CHICKENS

29

PART THREE:
SASKATOONS

49

PART FOUR:
CHOKECHERRIES

67

PART ONE

MOOSE MEAT

Aho,
Buddy can drop a bead on the sunrise
Stitch that right back up if he wanted
But really he just wants to see his kids
It's been a few weeks, up here in camp.
Kids back with their mom in the city
Good lady that hates the way he couldn't
Fulfill a promise to not end up like all the others
But a guy needs steady cash and kids
Need a hockey stick, PlayStation, clothes
Food, sports fees, trips back to the settlement
To see the grandparents, trips to Saskatoon
To see the aunties. Trips to Winnipeg to
Walk through the homelands and remember
That they're part of something more than
Whatever they learn in school.
Buddy's gonna bring them out to the bush
When he's on days off. He's gonna bring out
The old bolt action .22, the one that he got
From his dad, that his dad got from his dad
And that guy stole it from some drunk
White guy who bendered onto the road
Allowance and started yapping about women.
He got out easy just missing a gun and a
Couple teeth.
Buddy's gonna set up a bunch of pop cans
Let the kids plink away at them while he sits
Back and drinks steaming coffee coming out
Of the old Stanley, another gift from his dad.

Aho,
Fucking guy won't even text her back
At least not regularly and she knows
That he's got nothing but time on his hands
Because this camp runs an 8 and 8 and 8
No OT just a lot of downtime to get fat
Or get jacked. Scroll endlessly through
Social media to track back all the girls
That he might be texting, probably messaging
That lady, the apprentice, one who did
A couple camp stints and then decided
That serving at the BP's was more lucrative
Probably just looking for an easy out.
Fucking college websites don't make any sense.
She scrolls through programs. Can't understand
What these numbers mean, or how to just see
What the classes actually are. Wants to get some
Of her own cash and get the fuck out. At least
For a bit. Her sister used to post all these
Videos of her dancing and she got snagged up
By one of those Cree lawyers from Sask.
Now they live in Toronto and spend money
On trips, and drinks, and fancy dinners,
Not just Earl's happy hour and White Claws.
Could of done that shit too, but Buddy had a
Dream and he used to smell of campfire
Pine and sage. Moose meat frying in a pan.
Fucking guy, she tries to remember that smell.
He's probably texting the apprentice.

Aho,
Fancy University Boy, wears a collared shirt, distinguished.
Cheque came in from Rupertsland and he's gonna buy
Some textbook that costs about a quarter of what he paid
For his truck. White guy wrote it but acknowledges unceded
Territory but not Treaty where he's gonna read it.
Fancy University Boy's embarrassed about the truck he parks
At an aunty's place. She's a prof at the school.
Gave her a bunch of moose that Buddy and him hunted up
Last fall. Aunty Prof is happy because she gives it out to
All the students who need something to eat and there's a
Lot of them. Fancy University Boy wants to do something
Like that but he doesn't know jack shit about talking to
People and he doesn't know jack shit about how to be a
White guy and he doesn't know jack shit about how to do
Good in school. He used to get the highest grades back in
The town school, but that was just because he could read
And no one else could so the teachers who drove in from
The city on the daily said "ahh fuck it someone has to get
An A may as well be Fancy University Boy." And he got the A
And he still doesn't know jack shit. But that's about to change
When he gets this textbook and he swears that he's gonna
Read this one. He's gonna get invited to a fancy party where
People are gonna notice his collared shirt and he's not gonna
Say "gonna," he'll say "going to." And no one will comment on his
Accent. Every day, he practises saying his G's and turning
D's into T's. It'll come and he won't have to go home and
He'll move to the south side, date white women, read the textbook.

.

Aho,
Faculty meeting and they all turn to her
When someone gives a land acknowledgment
Staring. Waiting for some sort of validation.
The kind that relieves all the white guilt but
They still teach all sorts of old dead white problematic
Men and women and don't really give two shits
About all the students who drop out during
Shakespeare. And they want her to be everything
NDN. Decolonize my course package dropped on
Aunty Prof's desk and she's like *this isn't my fucking
Job* but she doesn't have tenure or status and the
Old white lady does and has a big say on if Aunty Prof
Can keep a job going. And she doesn't want to have
To apply to other universities because this one is home
Land, and the other ones don't have a prairie sunset
Turning rivers all sorts of pinks and purples. She wishes
She knew the Cree words for the colours because the
English ones don't do it justice. She thinks about her
Students and her future and all the shit she's gone
Through to get where she is and if any of it was worth
It. Those greys in her hair that came in hot when she
Was 25 working through a master's in a room full
Of shitty hipster bros who thought she owed them
Her body because she existed in their world. They tried in
Backrooms of faculty parties but some wimpy ass
Rich kid who studies poetry cannot keep
A thousand generations of matriarchal strength
Pinned down. And now she watches wimp boy get tenure
And dominate the meetings with land acknowledgments
And the right words. Always the right words. Couldn't fuck her
Physically so tries to do it mentally. And she sits back and
Knows that she'll never be anything but an
Angry Indian Aunty Prof.

Aho,
Buddy wakes up and he's got one last shift to hammer down
Before he can go home, grab the kids, and that BB gun.
Might be a couple swamp donkeys still sniffing butts in
The muskeg and he can round up a couple cousins
For a day or two to see if they can put one down, sage up
For the freezer. Take some over to see his kohkum who wrestles
The kids like she used to wrestle Buddy
Back when his dad would drop him off there on his way to
His own site. Buddy's banging away on pipe and thinking
Bout maybe grabbing some flowers for Baby Momma. Maybe
Head over to the Earl's on Jasper for happy hour, have a
Couple drinks and laugh like they used to, back before kid
Two, three, four, when she still smiled when she looked at him
Still laughed at his jokes. Still touched his arm. Wrapped
Herself under the faux Pendleton beside him, when Buddy
Could just feel love. Grab some flowers, Earl's happy hour
Doesn't know what else to do. He tells a joke and she shakes
Her head. Tells a story she ignores him. Goes hmm. Ask for
More money and he's got that thank god. But for how long who
Knows. He's worried that the work's all gonna get cut up.
How the hell does a welder get a job in this digital economy
He hears about from his hipster cousin who's shredding
Through a university degree and fancies himself mooniyaw.
Not Métis. This time Buddy's going to talk about his feelings
With Baby Momma. This time Buddy's going to ignore
The phone call from his boss asking him to put in another ten.
But he won't because he needs every little thing he can get
Because there's no room for him in the digital economy of the
Future.

Aho,
Baby Momma's got some cash from her sister.
TikTok royalties or something that she said could
Go towards her diploma after she spent a night
Crying into the phone. Baby Momma knows this
Is her sister's way of keeping her from Toronto.
Keeping her from her publicized Indigenized
Urban existence. Making videos about powwow
Dancing and smudging and watching the views
Roll in. Baby Momma goes by the bank and gets
A deposit slip just to know that it's real. Sister
Said she had to call up the Métis to see if they'd
Help pay for the rest but this would get her started.
She's got her own money. Not Buddy's. Not some
Sooniyaw from the mooniyaw. Not the kind of money
That attached to boys' bullshit like she had to deal with all the
Time when she was 18 and all she wanted
Was to survive. Before Buddy, before the kids niso,
Nisto, newo. She knows that Buddy would want five
And to keep going forever if it was up to him. But
It's not. She looks at the college website. Looks at
The Indigenous studies diploma program and laughs
Who the fuck would ever study being a half breed
Born into the slums of prairie poverty. She looks at the
Nursing one but can't get through the words in the intro
Looks through the childhood educator one and thinks
That's all she fucking does anyways. May as well
Get paid for it. Then Nisto pukes on Newo and it
All goes the way you think it would. What kind of
Baby Momma wants to escape her kids? Buddy better
Get off shift and take these units up to his kohkum's
Give her some time to go out to the karaoke bar with
Her friends and sing the version of Alanis Morissette
That she's been thinking about forever.

Aho,
Fancy University Boy bout to drop some knowledge
In this class if he could just stop shaking, even at the
Thought of raising his hand. He wants to add, be a part
But he can't stop his hands, and he can feel his face
Getting all flushed even though he hasn't had a sip of
Booze since his friend wandered off the bridge after
A bottle. No problem dropping knowledge when he's
By himself at home rehashing every single word that
He should of said while he drops into *Warzone* and
Yaps with his cousins back home about absolutely
Nothing and he loves the way that their words echo
Back through the headset and that he can feel connected
Even though he's four hundred clicks south. Fancy
University Boy figures a sweater vest will help him get
Through the shakes. Orders one from Gap and it
Arrives but feels like a stuffed cheddar smokie when he
Puts the vest on. He can't go bald. He's only 20 but
His hair won't stop winter dog shedding. What kind of Métis
Goes bald at 20? He calls his mom and asks her
About it and she says he's exaggerating but the high
Points are getting pretty pronounced and he heard some
Snickering in the workshop that he figures was about
Him. How do you fit in when everyone has everything
And all you got is a welder cousin who will throw you
The odd fifty here and there because he feels sorry for
You and you just want to ask him how he can just
Keep his head down and power through all the suck
That he has to go through on a daily?

Aho,
Standing up at the front of the class while they
All just stare, Aunty Prof wonders why she feels
The need to subject herself to the constant
"Well I don't really get it ... why don't they just
Get over it" and she can't believe that it's the 2020s
And she's still having that same fucking conversation
That she had in 2006 when she was trying to get
Through an undergrad and how everything has changed
And how nothing has changed. The little shit in
The front row claims to be Métis but hasn't dropped
Any sort of community lineage/claim/notification and
She knows she can't be the lady to tell little so-called
Métis shit that she shouldn't be appropriating identity
Because who knows. So she just drops lecture after
Lecture about those who've come before her. Buffy
Latimer, the Gills, so many minor professors and on
And on, and on, and on, and on, and on, and on, she
Thinks about PreteNDN lists and how she worried that
Her name was going to come up on one at some point
But then remembered that her granny would kick the
Shit out of anyone who said she wasn't Métis and she
Smiles and wants to cry because she misses her granny
So fucking much.

Aho,
Buddy never thought he'd get used to
Ignoring the northern lights but here he
Is working the night shift for the extra buck
And there they are whistling overhead.
He wouldn't dare though.
He hopes his kids don't dream of working
In the suck. That there's something better
Out there for them. The guys he works with
Down and out boys from the east and proud
Ol' prairie mutts, trace dignity through the
Pipe they thread together. Buddy traces
Dignity through the geese travelling along the
Milky Way. Hope is a dancing star in the dark
Night from cigarette embers even though it's
A non-smoking site. Buddy stares into the
Pressing darkness on the edges and tries to
Make out the shapes of the trees. Thinks
About his grandfather telling him of moose
Hunts back when that was survival for a winter
Or not. Back when that meant more than
Being told that you're not paid to think.
Dreams are a collective bitch and he hasn't
Had one in a long time.

Aho,
Baby Momma wants to smack the shit
Out of Niso but knows that that's not
The way to handle things even though
That's all she knew back in the day. And
If there's one thing she doesn't want it's to
End up like her fucking parents. She heard some
TikTok influencer talking about forgiveness
Once but she probably grew up in one of
Those new 100K combined salary professional
NDN homes. So she doesn't smack the shit
Out of Niso. Just cries a bit and wonders what
It would feel like to actually have Buddy at
Home, helping out with everything and not just
Parachuting in and buying the kids all
The gifts and spoiling the shit out of them for
Two weeks before disappearing and leaving
Her to hammer out discipline when all they
Ever do is tell her how much they hate her and
Love Buddy. She wants to be the fun one.
Her friend from the drop-in centre at the library
Told her to go into the Indigenous Student Centre
At the college and chat with the ladies in there.
Said they're real gems. Lived it. Not some of
These white women who are thinking that they're
Native because they went to a ceremony once
Where the self-appointed elder promised them
Spirituality in exchange for blowjobs. Same women
Who tattoo feathers behind their ears and spit venom
When she showed up to the community ceremonies
With Niso, Nisto, Newo fighting and screaming and
She's just fucking trying. Okay?

Aho,
Holy fuck she's smart and beautiful and definitely
Out of his league but he's gonna try to write something
Reaalll deadleh for the workshop and she'll hear his
Words and be like, wow Fancy University Boy isn't a
Stuffed-up moose sausage, jalapeño goose smokie
He's a real gem. So edgy that one. Thinks real deep
Thoughts and doesn't spend most of every day spinning
In circles and pacing back and forth. Can't drop out because
Then he's just back home and he can't go back home
Because then he's just another fucking guy who couldn't
Cut it in the city. Fancy University Boy remembers when he
Accidentally walked into a door at a house party and someone
Yelled, "guess they don't teach you how to use a doorknob in
University there college boy," and those words have never left
Him. He still doesn't know if he really understands doorknobs
Or why things need to be closed off. He doesn't
Want to lose his options. Doesn't want to stop thinking but he
Remembers having opinions and if there's one thing these
Fucking classes have done it's take everything that he thought
He ever knew and flip it upside down so the only opinion that
He has right now is that he's just sad. How do you express
Something that no one in your family has ever expressed before?
How do you say, "I'm not okay?" He wanted to be a high school
Teacher because that's the only career he knew existed outside of
Social worker. Too dumb for law or medical school. Too angry to be
A social worker. Too illiterate to know the difference between "to" and
"Too" and the proper time and place to use them. He writes a poem
About being cocky and confident and reads it while he clicks the top
Of a pen, clickclickclickclickclickclickclickclickclick, shaking now. One
Of his workshop crushes grabs the pen out of his hand and tells him to
Stop that and just read.

Aho,
Why does she have to sit on every committee.
Why can't the white lady who wants to engage
The community take the initiative to actually go
And find someone and pay them to be a part of
The community process. But here's Aunty Prof
Sitting in her shared office. Accessible and lacking
Any sort of structural support that will back her
Up in saying no to stupid requests. *Let me guess
Another study about what's wrong with the NDN.*
Lady asks her, "what about we get all the residential
School survivors together so they can share their
Testimonies?" And Aunty Prof wants to scream because
They fucking did that exact thing a decade ago with the
TRC! But this lady's much too lazy to know that, even though
She's an expert on Indigenous literatures. Way more
Of an expert than Aunty Prof (at least if you're comparing
Salaries). Her friends have scattered and she would love
To be able to go to someone's house and drink three
Bottles of wine and collectively know that this is all
So fucking stupid with an actual peer collective. But
A long time will pass until the next conference and
Her shitty salary doesn't afford her flights out to Toronto.
She didn't think 30 would feel this lonely. She loses
Herself in books by Black writers and when her colleagues
Ask her what she's reading for "fun" she tells them and
They can't believe that she's not reading the latest hits of
Indigiliterature, but honestly, it all fucking hits way too close to
Home.

Aho,
Another one gone. Buddy watches the posts
Start up on Instagram and the GoFundMe kick
Up. He tosses five hundred bucks at it and knows
That he'll hear about it from Baby Momma when
They "talk" tonight. She'll see his name on the
Donation list. Another One Gone. Another kid
Growing up without her dad. Buddy remembers
When they used to run around in the back alleys
And storm drainage ditches of the tiny prairie city
Of their childhood. Putting pennies on railroad tracks.
Putting crayfish into an underwater ring made of rocks
Hoping they'd wrestle like Stone Cold Steve Austin and
The Rock did on the videos they'd rent from the store.
Same store that kept change in old film canisters for the
Neighbourhood kids to use. Buddy misses the funeral
Watches the tribute video when it gets uploaded online.
Has to click through a few ads about financial success to
Get to it. Buddy doesn't understand crypto and doesn't
Give a shit about it. But according to all his co-workers
They're going to be retired next year and Buddy is going
Still slugging it up. The tribute video has a photo
From the local newspaper: Buddy, Another One Gone, and
Buddy's brother are all wearing baggy jeans with chain
Wallets and T-shirts over long sleeves, holding up frogs
They caught. Buddy starts crying and then stops because
He's in the F-550 waiting for the pipefitters to get their shit
Done so he can drop a bead. If they saw him sitting in here
Shedding tears it would all be over. He restarts the video, exits
An ad. Watches again. "Against the Wind" is playing as the photos
Slide through and Buddy wishes that he knew Another One Gone
In their adult days. He wishes his brother wasn't done in
Over a decade ago by a quad crash when his bucket-less dome
Smacked into the concrete. And that was that. Text comes in
Did you seriously just give $500 to some fucking fundraiser?

Aho,
Baby Momma signs Peyak and Niso up for a summer
Day camp program at the library. Same free city-sponsored
Ones that she went to when she was running wild around
The Avenue in baggy-ass white T-shirt, shorts, and a pink hat
That some kid called her gay for wearing. And she
Thought that it meant stupid so she cried and cried and cried
By herself in the back corner of the library with her stupid hat
On and a *Baby-Sitters Club* novel in hand. Same kid called her
Gay later when she went to check those books out to bring home.
Heard the camp counsellor who was probably some 20-year-old
Working a shit job for the summer snigger at her. She banded up
With her sister and the two of them swam circles in the legislature
Fountain not knowing that a hundred years before, their family had
Signed an adhesion to Treaty 6 not far from where they stood. Not
Knowing that their ancestors' blood and tears ran into the soil and that
The marble structure towering over their fountain was just a symbol
Of a future that didn't include a coupla Métis kids splashing in a
Fountain. She drops Peyak and Niso off and doesn't think twice about
Them. They can handle themselves. Picks them up end of the day
And hears from the staff all about how Peyak beat up some kid who
Called Niso a "prairie n*****." She says *good*. And they all drive home.
No more camp. Some things change and some things don't. Tries to
Call up Buddy but he's not picking up. Sends a vague text that he's
Pulling a double. Doesn't believe for a second that he is. Baby Momma
Sheds a different type of tear than she did back when she was just a
Kid, worries about what the future will look like for all of them.

Aho,
Fancy University Boy wrote a short story for his class and
It's the greatest thing that anyone in the history of humanity
Has ever written. Just put the keyboard down a couple
Seconds ago and oh boy this one is the ticket to greatness.
He probably won't even have to finish up the semester just
Strut right into some literary hall of fame somewhere get a
Wikipedia page in his name. He doesn't even bother
With a copy edit before he submits it into the Blackboard
Portal that's the closest to internet history that he'll
Ever use. Wonders if this will get him noticed enough to
Build up confidence enough to stop his hand from shaking,
To stop the darkness from coming when he thinks about
Responding in class, to get him a date not that he even
Knows what a date really is. But it sounds like something
From a book he reads. This is the story. A couple days
Later in the workshop the prof pulls him aside and asks
Him if he could define plagiarism for him. Fancy University
Boy says it's when you steal something and it hasn't clicked
That he's in big fucking shit. But the prof is prepared to make
A deal because he understands the circumstances that
Created the situation that Fancy University Boy is in and
How the intergenerational trauma that he's experiencing
From his family's involvement in the residential school system
Clouds his judgement when it comes to the academy
And how the transition from an Indigenous world view to a Western
One sometimes is its own form of trauma. Wonders if Fancy
University Boy doesn't think he would be better off writing something
That speaks to the trauma within his community and how to
Overcome it with, he doesn't know, maybe a cultural moment?
He tells Fancy University Boy to write about the powwow dancing
That he does? Grass Dance? Chicken? Fancy University Boy
Nods along. He doesn't tell him that he's never gone to a powwow.
The prof will give him an opportunity to hand in a story
That isn't stolen, unravels a laundry list of poverty porn to check

Out. And Fancy University Boy walks home, loads up the online Class registration portal and withdraws from the class. Getting that Big old fancy W.

Aho,
She got passed up for the promotion again and it's
Got an eerie ring to the three times that she went
Before the dissertation committee, before they found
Her work compelling enough to put a Dr. in front of her name
And a PhD after it. She spent a year with an old boy
Out on a rez and he told her that it's all just a big circle
They can't see it but we sure can, and our circles are
Different. But still she doesn't know if she'll ever get
To the next step. Sure Aunty Prof has made it already
In their eyes and should just be happy to be one of the
"Good ones" who are breaking through the stereotypes
And she thinks about all the people she knows who aren't
Stereotypes but just live to live and support their kids and
Friends and family and never think twice about work when
They go home at the end of the day. Someone told her
Once that it's heartwork but she doesn't get why every NDN
Within the academy needs to go full warrior at the end. Why
Can't we all just sit and create a better future? But the tomahawks
Are out and it's 1860s Prairies up in this bitch.
She wants to walk off the campus, borrow a canoe from one
Of the Bumble boys that she unfortunately dates. The white
Ones without the fish but with the canoe paddles, the NDN
Fetish, playing colonizer through their understanding of her
Feelings. She feels old and she wonders when she got so
Jaded. So she goes on another date and the entire time she
Thinks about stealing his canoe and paddling off into the
Abyss of northern Saskatchewan lakes but she hasn't spent
A night in a tent since she went to a culture program in her
Master's and at the end of the day loves sleeping solo in the
King-sized bed. Aunty Prof wonders if it's not love that she craves
And she analyzes how pitiful all the white boys look when she
Fucks and then destroys them. It's not really a form of
Land Back. But maybe it is?

PART TWO

PRAIRIE CHICKENS

Aho,
Buddy packs up his bag. Tries to get the mud
Off his boots but that ain't happening anytime
Soon. Dons his last clean pair of underwear
The ones that he saved just for the trip home.
He's going back to Amiskwaciy and he's gonna
Hug the hell out of his kids. Probably get an earful
From Baby Momma but who knows maybe this
Time it'll be different. They used to fly them in and
Out of site but shit's different now. Goddamn NDP
Ruined Alberta oil for good. At least according to
Everyone. Buddy just agrees, he really doesn't care
Or think about those kind of things. Just wants to
Not get in a car crash on the ten-hour drive from the
Suck back to the city. Dreams of the lights of downtown
Reflecting off of the north side. Maybe snagging through
Kingsway and sneaking in an extra perogy/kueby from
The good Ukrainian place. Baby Momma doesn't leave
The light on when he pulls into the driveway next to
Her Toyota 4Runner. The one with all the stick figures, dogs
Hearts, and words drawn into the dust by the kids. He thinks
For a second that maybe they all stayed up to surprise
Him but that ain't happening. Just babes. He opens up
The bedroom doors and gives Peyak, Niso, Nisto big
Kisses on their foreheads while they dream, he hopes
Of beautiful birds flying low under sunrises and the smell
Of their kohkum's moose stew, the recipe with the red wine
And the bay leaves. Newo wakes up and Buddy picks her
Up from her crib and she just keeps screaming louder. He
Tries to rock her back to sleep and Baby Momma comes
Storming into the bedroom and yells, "what are you doing?
Leave her alone!" and Buddy realizes that unfortunately that's
All he's ever done. Baby Momma takes Newo and Newo stops
Crying, shoots a glare at Buddy that brings him to the floor.
He goes up to the two of them and Baby Momma turns her

Back on him and walks into the next room. Buddy stares
After her and tries to find the right words to tell her how much
She means to him and how he just wants to acknowledge the
Work that she puts in with the kids. He scrambles and tries
To force out the words but a bullet blocks his throat.

Aho,
She knows that Buddy is the kind of guy who will
Keep the child support coming. And honestly, is
It really *that* different now that he doesn't technically
Live with them? Baby Momma dreams of a future when
She can just cut herself off from him. Cut herself off
From everyone and everything and the kids are moved
Off and she's Instagram famous laying on a beach
Somewhere in the south where the water turns turquoise
Instead of brown. She knew that it was never going to
Change and she's pretty proud of herself for kicking
Buddy out. Not something that a previous version of her
Would have ever done. And she smiles deep but
Doesn't like the idea of him being happy, not yet at least
Talks to her friend about setting up an online dating
Profile but the last time she went on any of those sites
Plenty of Fish was still kicking. Tries to find the right
Selfie, but doesn't like the way that her face looks just
Like her mother's and aunties'. *When did that happen*
She wonders as she tries to suck her cheeks in but
It doesn't matter, she dreams forever of how she looked
When she was 22 and a couple months out from
Getting pregnant with Peyak. She doesn't know about
Peyak and Niso, they seem to look more like Buddy
Every day. They carry his weight. But the younger two
Nisto and Newo, have her eyes and that's all that matters.
She thought back then that the love of children could
Save her and listened hard when people told her that
They were a gift from the creator and she doesn't regret
A thing but things could also be a lot different. Or maybe
They'd be the same. Who knows. She started sneaking
Out after the kids go to sleep for a CBD cigarette, something
Without nicotine but a ritual to keep her thinking straight.
She's nervous about the upcoming semester and wonders if
She's going to be that old lady in the class. Doesn't know

How she's going to afford daycare and doesn't want to
Call on her family. That wouldn't be much different than
Calling in a bear to take care of the kids. Could be great
Could be terrifying. But hell hasn't this life been nothing but
One choice after the other.

Aho,
Fancy University Boy finds himself walking in circles
Around downtown smoking used cigarette butts thinking
About what he's going to do in a month when the grades
Get sent back to the funders and they realize that it's
All W's across the board and the rent cheque stops
Coming. Will he move back to the north, or can he kick it
Long enough in the city? But he doesn't know how to
Work except for that stint pumping gas at the Husky.
But even that job is obsolete now, and no one has any use
For a kid who can't even tell his own story. Gets invited to
A party and drinks enough to make an ass of himself
Trying to steal a poster from a wall. Gets a message on
Facebook the next day about it and he ignores it long enough
To end up at another party where some kid from his workshop
Attacks him after an exchange of insults and he throws the
Kid through the glass door because even if you're a
Fancy University Boy the north teaches you how to fuck
Someone up when you need to. Wakes up covered in the
Kid's blood and a Facebook message from him asking him
To pay for the glass. Which you better believe isn't going
To happen. Time in the city starts to squawk like the magpies
On death row and he can't get over the jitters from whiskey.
Walks the bridge home thinks about the ice below and if any
Of the floes make it back to Montreal. Gets a job working in
A warehouse where after a couple weeks he can hop on the
Forklift and he learns that story doesn't matter anymore, just
Get those fucking oil field parts loaded up or shit's gonna hit
The fan and spray all over his future.

Aho,
Course evaluations come in and too many of them focus
On the way she dresses and apparently her beaded earrings
Which were a "distraction" and "trying to make her Indigenous."
She wonders if other profs have to deal with comments on their
Appearance or if they're able to just focus on learning and teaching.
One doesn't like the PowerPoint template she used, and one thinks
That she should accommodate the white cishet men as they're
"Having a real rough go right now." Aunty Prof wishes she could light
Them up. But all she can do is ignore the fact that they'll use this against
Her the next time she tries to gain any sense of permanency.
What would it be like back working for community? She's smart enough
To know that it's not this imagined paradise. But then the drama is at
Least NDN drama, and no one gives a shit about tokenizing/fetishizing
You. She turns on Instagram and ignores the add requests from her
Students and the info memes that are constantly pounding into her head
That the world fucking sucks. But if these people haven't figured that out
Already then what hope do they really have for the future.
If she donated to every cause that flashed for sixty seconds on her
Screens she'd turn into a cause herself. And that's not something
She's willing to do. But she's not sure what she's willing to do if it
Means that she's got another forty years of this white shit. Whoever thought
That being an academic was a better career than working the River
Cree table-game scene never took home the tips.

Aho,
Buddy's got a hot date tonight, Dene lady who just moved to the city
From Saskatchewan and doesn't seem to have any connection whatsoever
To Baby Momma, though he knows that if they get to a point where they
Really start digging then something will come up. It always does.
But shit, Baby Momma hasn't talked to him in months, just grunts at him
When he swings by to pick the kids up on the odd weekend when she's got
Plans and he imagines that those plans involve lots of other men but he can't
Say shit, just bites his tongue because he wants to see the kids and he knows
That she's got all the power to make that go away in a flash and he doesn't
Want to just end up like that fucking guy. The guy everyone already thinks he is.
Hotshot who delivers the pipe to site loves to make cracks and Buddy wants
To weld his lips shut. But everyone on site loves to pretend that they don't
Give a fuck about their kids, exes, and current lovers. But Buddy does.
Sometimes he tells the crew that he's going off to drop a bush shit and he
Just walks into the woods and sits down, lights a cigarette, and sobs silently
For a couple minutes before throwing his sunnies back on and coming back
To a world that's trying to suck the last drops of dinosaur blood out of the earth.
He hopes that the Dene lady is going to become a current lover, he hasn't had
One of those in a long fucking time. Since Baby Momma still held him to her
Chest when he got home from these long shifts. Back when she still believed
In him. Buddy thinks about Dene Lady a lot and he's never even met her in real
Life. She told him on Bumble that she liked his photo where he was holding up
A big bag of Costco chicken strips in the classic fish photo pose. Thought that
Was real funny. He told her he had lots of jokes. He doesn't, but she said he
Could buy her a drink and they could play some darts. Buddy's worried she's
Gonna go running when she finds out about Peyak, Niso, Nisto, Newo, but also
Dreams about the six of them sitting down at BP's with the kids ripping through
Colouring sheets, a couple Great White Norths on the table, some Cactus
Cuts and unlimited pop. They're all laughing all the time in his head. Having such
A good time that he doesn't have to think about the way Baby Momma's eyes
Looked for the last year of their life together.

Aho,

Baby Momma is looking fucking good. Every single guy she swipes right on ... IT'S A MATCH. She knew those photos were gonna find her someone with a Cute smile and one of those white boy messy haircuts, the kind where they're All still put together, not some rat nest like Buddy had most of the time when He took his hat off. She swipes left on bald men out of principle but her Cree Language teacher told her once that bald men were considered the most holy Back in the day because they were closer to the creator. She does laugh a little Bit about that and then swipes left. Fuck em. She's got her mind set on a guy Who wears colourful dress socks. A guy with a white collar job who comes Home at 4:30 every single night with a little gift and eyes only for her. Who Plays with Peyak, Newo, Niso, Nisto and understands how to role model what It truly means to commit to parenting. Shows them how to show emotion. The Podcast that her sister sent her said that she should only date men who are Strong enough to go to therapy. That sounded like some Toronto shit to her, He'll just take someone who talks about something that isn't just the day-to-day. IT'S A MATCH. She stares at the picture of a guy with a backwards Jays cap on Shirtless on a boat with a beer in hand smiling the pearly whites of Intergenerational money and she doesn't know what to say so she just scrolls On to the next IT'S A MATCH. Some guy wearing a suit on a balcony of a High-rise looking out over the downtown of some city that definitely isn't Prairie with a sense of accomplishment, entitlement, rich shit and she keeps Scrolling. Next guy's standing with two good-looking dogs in a field looks a bit More normal but then he's not wearing a hat in the next photo and she has to Swipe left. She checks her messages and scrolls down through the sup's, hey's, Hi's, what you doing tonight, down to fuck?, you into threesomes, gonna fuck You hard tonight, hey fatso suck this dick ... to the one that asks her if she has Kids. She types a smiley face back and says hey! How's it going! I do, I love Them so much, they mean the world to me. And she sees the text bubbles Boiling at the bottom and she's got a little stomach flutter happening. Then the Next message comes back. I'm gonna fuck you while they watch. She drops the Phone and lets out a noise, something between a cry and a heart breaking in Real time.

Aho,

Sometimes Fancy University Boy gets to drive the delivery truck
When the hotshot guys are fucking up. He likes to hit up the Papaschase
Industrial district warehouse at the end of his run before he rips out to
The sites to deliver the rods, flanges, whatever. The boys who work
The forklifts like to fuck around with beers after shift and he likes to
Dummy a few and have a couple smokes before he hits the long road
West or north, direction depending on the EcOnOmY. He likes to
Shoot the shit with the guys who work the forks, and he'll leave when they
Start giving him all hell about being a Fancy University Boy. Fucking kid
Thought he could go to school, what kind of idiot would want to do that
When you can make good bank behind a wheel or in a warehouse? Idiot.
Some people got it like the boys in the warehouse and some people don't.
Started calling him Fancy Hotshot Boy and that shit stuck like a truck in
Spring breakup. Fancy Hotshot Boy just takes his dues even though the
Other boys told him to shrink his degree down and get that shit printed
Out on his hardhat. He tried to tell them that he didn't have a degree,
Just did a couple semesters but that flew right over their heads. When
The funding got cut off, he moved into a bedroom of a townhouse that one
Of the warehouse boys bought when he won the 50/50 at the Oilers game
One night. Other guy that split the pot apparently dropped his half that same
Night at the rippers and then a blizzard back at a penthouse suite at the
River Cree.

Aho,
Aunty Prof got the big job offer. Tenure track all the way out in
The Golden Horseshoe. Which is pretty much fucking Sweden for
All she can tell and even though it would be nice to get the fuck out of
This university scene a quick Google search shows the majority
Of the faculty are Ontario/Quebec-based Métis and anyone in their
Right mind knows that you want to stay far away from those
Kinda people. They'll eat up your family story and regurgitate it with
A trauma twist, brown contacts, and black hair dye for their white
Audience that applauds their resilience. She chokes on that word
Who the fuck wants resiliency when all you want is to be able to
Live a life outside of the confines put in place by a system that will
Never give an inch. So she's not going to take it and she's going to
Continue to teach a crazy course load but just below the benefit line.
But something has to change or she's gonna drown in the tears of
The white saviours who are here to bring her piety, oh she's such a
Warrior. The princess they always dreamt of from their Western fantasy
Novels and she wishes that she had that cold hard steel iron that her
Aunties can bring to the table and shut down the prying questions with
A single fucking look.

Aho,
Date went real deadly, all sorts of deadly, ever deadly
What do those northern boys always say with the real
Thick rez accent? The one that sounds like there's a moose
Snorting along with the words? But Dene Lady is beautiful
And she's real short like all those Dene ladies, and she's got
A good job. Just moved back to the city from doing some schooling
Down in Vancouver at Native Education College and now she's
Doing some curriculum or something like that. Buddy didn't really
Get what she was talking about and she didn't really expect him to
Which he appreciated. She said she just wants a funny guy who
Isn't too messy. None of that drama shit for her. No public Facebook/
Instagram call-outs that she better step the fuck up if she's gonna
Be messing with someone's baby daddy. And Buddy laughs and hopes
To all hell that Baby Momma hates him as much as she says she does
And doesn't want shit to do with him. Because Dene Lady is a real one
And he'd like to play darts and listen to her sing Tracy Chapman's
"Fast Car" at the karaoke night on the Avenue over and over and over
Again.

Aho,
Baby Momma sits down in the classroom and she's feeling all sorts of
Inferiority. Everyone who's sitting around her is looking all smartass with
Their fancy laptops and notebooks and bags that look like they belong in
A college classroom. And Baby Momma took a couple of the notebooks
That Peyak and Niso didn't fully use last year in school and she ripped out
The ten pages or so that they did, so now she's got some child scribbles on
The front of the Hilroy and a couple haggard Mr. Sketches that don't smell
Anymore to "highlight" things with. Since when did you need to do everything
Online as a student? Baby Momma doesn't have a computer and the ones that
Are for student use in the Indigenous Student Centre are always in use.
She asks the instructor if she can handwrite the assignments out and the kid who
Looks younger than her just blinks. So confused as to what handwriting could
Even be. She does her best not to break down into tears throughout the first
Days. Does her best not to fully just walk the fuck out. Does her best not to
Try and fight someone and understands that her immediate response is to get
Violent. If you hurt someone they can't hurt you and that little bitch that sits in
The front row that she remembers from a parenting program they try and force
All the Métis moms into when they leave the hospital was snarky then, continues
To be snarky now. But then the two of them go to Tim's on the break and get
A couple steeped teas and Baby Momma realizes that this lady is doing the
Same thing she is. They smoke a cigarette together even though Baby Momma
Doesn't really do that anymore but she thinks a friend is a friend and doesn't
Feel like crying as much as she did whenever the instructors or the advisers or
Anyone who speaks the language that she doesn't understand says Something.

Aho,

Fancy University Boy and some of the boys from the warehouse
Are going out on Whyte, gonna meet some women and have some
Smokes and drinks and probably a couple slices from Steel Wheels
Late night and Fancy University Boy is pretty fired up that he's been
Invited out with the older dudes to have a good time. These boys got
Cars and stories and seem to be pretty tied into the whole warehouse
Scene in a cool way. Who the fuck would go to university when this
Whole world plays out in a godsend? And Fancy University Boy has
Forklift skills that the old boys respect. Say he could pick a penny up
And drop it down a stripper's butt crack with a lift, that's how
Accurate he is. Fancy University Boy kinda hopes that the night might
End up there. He's never been to the rippers and he hasn't seen a
Boob since eleventh grade, when Brit and him made out in the
Laundry room of his friend's parent's trailer back on the settlement. She
Didn't talk to him after that night and when he told his friends that they
Had fooled around she denied it, which stung a lot back then but he
Doesn't think too much about it now. Especially since it's fucking ON
Tonight with the boys. And they're walking down Whyte Ave and some
Frat boys with white T-shirts are coming towards them and the one guy
Says to him ... "nice hairline bud." And they keep going, throw a couple
More fuck yous to each other. But Fancy University Boy is crushed.
He thought he was looking pretty good, and all of a sudden he's feeling
Like everyone in the whole world is just staring at his head and wondering
Why he's going bald. And he pretends to go out to get some cigarettes
And peaces the fuck back to his apartment.

Aho,
Aunty Prof didn't take the job. Gonna stick it out in the motherland
For another semester of an overloaded teaching schedule that takes
Advantage of her time without any hope for promotion now that she's
Firmly established as someone who needs to teach, because there are
Bills to pay and unfortunately a PhD in Indigenous literatures isn't
Going to get her anywhere but strutted out for the institution. She
Wonders about the students who sit through her classes, not the ones
With the confidence that beam in discussion, and throw perfectly
Crafted thoughts back at her about the eloquence of decolonial narrative
Thought when it concerns modern Indigenous perspectives on writing
Outside of the Western gaze. But the ones who sit in the back with
Nothing to add to the discussion besides their own associated trauma
Experiences that she doesn't want to drudge up in a classroom because
That's just fucking wrong. And the students start dropping out
Towards mid-November when the daylight's done and everyone sits
In darkness through afternoon classes, where the only light is that
Hopefully some of these students make the world a better place.
She wonders about those who she sees for a couple weeks
Who write one beautiful paper and then disappear after she compliments
Their critical analysis and ability to craft a thoughtful piece around
A community-centred Indigenous lens. The ones who disappear without
An email, a conversation, a dialogue, anything to give her a sense of
Where they go. Because she worries. Too many people are gone.

Aho,
Buddy kicks his Stoner Cousin out of the duplex for the night.
Gives him fifty bucks and tells him to go out and hit up the foosball
Tables over at the neighbourhood pub, and Stoner Cousin hightails
It over there like a man on a mission. Stoner Cousin has a crush on
The mom of the three-generation server family that works the pub and
Lives over in the low-income housing that they rent the duplex in …
Well Stoner Cousin technically rents the duplex because he qualifies
And Buddy is on the edge, especially with all the payments to
Baby Momma on the regular but that shit ain't going to matter tonight
Because Dene Lady is coming over and Buddy has a plan. He's going
To cook up that moose stew recipe that his aunty taught him years ago
The old specialty, you know some red wine in the mix to give it a bit of
Touch, what the normal NDN stews lack. Makes that shit classy.
Then Buddy is going to invite her up to the balcony to watch the sunset
Over the Hazy-D school fields, good view. And hey, balcony's attached to
The bedroom, so who knows … maybe shit will progress. Buddy's pretty
Excited about the idea. Feels like it's been a long time since he's had
Anyone interested in him, anyone who thinks he's got a good story and
Laughs at his jokes, anyone who he feels some sort of connection with.
Someone to cook a meal for … he hasn't done that in a while, been living
Off the prepackaged dinners and the takeout runs with Stoner Cousin
So it'll be a nice change to have someone beautiful around to laugh and
Tell stories to over a good bowl of moose stew. Buddy hasn't been this
Fired up in a long time.

Aho,
Baby Momma likes the prof in her one class. Guy's probably her age
And speaks so well about the nuances of Treaty and Indian Acts and
All this shit that she's never thought of before but kind of checks out
But she's a bit worried that when the unit comes up around the Sixties
Scoop that it's gonna drum up one of those memories that she's
Been trying to push down. The whole lifestyle that she's been trying to
Switch for a couple generations for Peyak, Niso, Nisto, Newo, for herself.
But it's her favourite class, the one that they make all the NDN students
Who come in on the bridging program take, Indigenous Student Success
Or some bullshit like that. They only make the NDN kids take it, pay an
Extra couple hundred bucks, but as the prof says, it should really be the
Rest of the college that takes the class. Ain't no one need to teach an
NDN how to NDN. But he says that and Baby Momma knows that she
Doesn't know shit about any of what he's talking about. Not like anyone
She's ever known is talking about the nuances of Métis scrip and how
That system fucked over the prairie governance structures in Métis
Communities for all time. At least until the next revolution that prof likes
To hint at. But Baby Momma doesn't think that prof has the vibe to truly
Lead a revolution and that's why she likes him. Someone who's smart
And even if he isn't going to be the leader at least he's got the ambition
To try and create a better future. Baby Momma hasn't had a crush in a
Long time and she finds herself getting nervous before class. Almost makes
Her want to step back and not go to class. Drop out. Forget the whole
Thing. But it's also the only reason she finds herself at the college. Not that
That makes sense but Baby Momma also doesn't think it makes sense that
She's even here to begin with!

Aho,
Fancy University Boy can't stop eyeing up his hairline.
And the way that every time he takes a shower it seems
Like the drain is just plugging up the entire time with what's
An endless cascade of hair falling off his head and ain't
Nothing growing back up there. Who the fuck goes bald this
Early? And he's stressing the fuck out because he couldn't
Meet a girl beforehand and now he definitely isn't going to
Meet anyone and all he wants to do is meet someone, it's
All he fucking thinks about all day every day when he's ripping
Forks around the shop. And the boys there don't have
Girlfriends but that doesn't need to be him, but they have exes
And at this point he'd even take an ex just to have the experience
Of having a girlfriend in the first place. They at least have that.
Fancy University Boy doesn't have shit. Not a memory. Not a
Feeling. Daydreams a bit too hard and drops a pallet loaded up
With flanges off of the top shelf and shit goes clattering all over
Almost takes out the guy who's working with him and he's like
"What the fuck is going on?" Yells at Fancy University Boy like he's
Never gotten yelled at before and the rest of the shop is over there
Doing the same thing and all he wants to do is go crawl back in a
Corner and fucking have that pallet full of flanges fall on his head
And end this whole fucking thing that's been going on for way too
Long. First time he thinks about a way out and the feeling is a bit
Too comfortable. Real fucking comfortable.

Aho,
Aunty Prof needs to get drunk and fuck on a beach
Books herself an adult-only, all-inclusive trip down to
Mexico. Makes sure it's not one of the reeeealllll
Adult-only ones. But just one without kids. She's had
Enough of them, even though most of the ones she
Teaches are in their late teens / early twenties. But enough
Of that, she's gonna go sit in her bikini by the pool and
Read that book *Prairie Edge* that she's meant to
Get through for a long time but just can't because of the
Sheer suckpile of student writing and constant emails
That she has to go through on a daily basis. She's been
Hitting up these HIIT running classes by the basement
Suite she rents. Never seen another NDN in one of them
But that's all right, the lady who runs it blasts remixed Weezer
And Taylor Swift and that theme song from *White Lotus* that
Gets everyone running their asses off, anxiety-laced drama
But it actually got her thinking that she needs a fucking break.
Because she hasn't had one in a while and no matter what she's
Not going to talk about her stupid-ass job, or her stupid-ass classes
Or her stupid ass ... fuck, she looks fucking great. Best shape she's
Been in since she didn't have to think about that anymore
And she's gonna wear the hell out of that bikini.
Isn't even gonna pack anything else.
Maybe some condoms. Maybe not.

PART THREE

SASKATOONS

Aho,
Dene Lady comes by and Buddy thinks she looks like
The fucking northern lights dancing around the full moon when
She comes in the door and he's smiling and happy and cooking
Showing off that he's an organized adult by having everything
Fucking cleaned up already. He's wearing a casual shirt and thinking
That he's looking pretty good, cooking it up in the kitchen and
Place is looking all clean cause he kicked Stoner Cousin's ass
To help him with it before he sent him off to the foosball tables.
And Dene Lady, god she's got this purple dye in her hair that reflects
Back in the backlit mirror in a certain light and Buddy can't get
Enough of it. They start eating and telling jokes and stories and
He talks a bit about his family and she talks about hers and she
Makes a lot of jokes which Buddy loves and he tries to laugh
Appropriately. She tells him his moose stew is decent and compliments
The wine that he used in it and now they're drinking on the side
But she doesn't have much just a little glass here and there. Buddy's
Thinking that this is going well, too well, and they finish up and head
Up to watch a prairie sunset. Which always fucking rips. They watch
And keep chatting. Dene Lady tells a joke about getting naked and
Buddy takes that as his cue to move in for a kiss and their lips touch
And he's fucking fired up. Kisses her again and she's not really putting
Anything into it. Buddy moves back a bit and she goes, "uhh I don't
Know if I'm really feeling this." Buddy pulls back. Dene Lady starts talking
Real fast and the words are flying by him a bit and he's a bit confused
Thought things were going well and she says something about how he
Didn't kiss her when she came in the door, isn't really into it, might be
Her mood, maybe the next day she'll feel different. Buddy's spinning a
Bit. She looks at him and he sees that purple reflection in her hair and
The northern lights fading out from the city glow creeping in. She tells
Him that she's going to go and he walks her out.
Stunned, not quite sure what the fuck just happened, she's gone and he's
Sitting there looking at their dishes, dirty in the perfectly clean kitchen and
The lipstick on her wine glass.

Aho,
Baby Momma's got a paper due but she can't find the time
To sit down and write it, what with the kids just fucking givin'
Er in the cry department and anytime she cracks a book one
Of them is hitting the other one or someone's falling off of a
Table or hungry or shitting themselves and she wonders how
Anyone gets through fucking school if they have all of these
Little hellions distracting her on a moment's notice. And lord
She loves them but sometimes it takes all of her strength not
To pick one of them up by the leg and start Bowser-swinging
Them into the other kids until they're all quiet. Someone told
Her to just give them some iPads but who the hell can afford
Those and who the hell thinks that the little baby can play on
An iPad and what advice is that really anyways? She
Wonders about calling up Buddy to see if he'd come over and
Just hang out with the kids for a bit. But it's been a while now
And she ain't messaging his sorry ass cause she doesn't want
To give him some sort of idea that she misses him because
He truly doesn't even cross her mind that often anymore.
Enjoys that there's one less thing to worry about. She listens
To these podcasts that talk about what went wrong in a relationship
And how to learn for the next one and they're all from some
Rich-ass white girl perspective. And what did she really learn
Except that rich bitches don't get knocked up before they go
Back to school. She wonders if this was really the right idea.
The right place. The right thing to do. The right time. Maybe
It's not her that elevates but rather the kids who are way too
Goddamn smart for their own good.

Aho,
Fancy University Boy is out of a job. Wasn't the safety incident
Everyone got shitcanned. Something about Trudeau ruining the
Economy and oil going in the shitter because they can't build a
Goddamn pipeline without some libtards getting involved. At least
That's what the boss told the boys in the warehouse. Kept a skeleton
Crew of the old guard on. And the rest of them, well, fuck Trudeau.
Fancy University Boy is dead-ass broke, more than broke, he owes
The settlement his tuition repayments for dropping out of school and
He's got nothing to his name. Doesn't think about girls anymore though
He's got other problems than that, and he doesn't want to move back
Home to hear about another failure. Spends his days wandering
Around downtown, asks for jobs in a bunch of different restaurants and
Bars and none of them have anything for him, none of them have anything
For anyone. Until he just happens to wander by a pub on the south side
Of the river with a dishwasher who went full apeshit on the tail end of a meth
Binge and they need someone stat for the fucking upcoming dinner
Rush and he's in the pit scrubbing burger grease and ketchup streaks
Off white plates. He nods at the one NDN cook working the line and
The cook gives him a not-fucking-here look so he keeps his head down
And inhales nacho crumb dust and guacamole steam.

Aho,
Aunty Prof met some chump in the airport who said he had
Upgrade credits to burn and she's not quite sure what that
Means but she's sitting in business class which is something
That she's never done before. And the free champagne is flowing.
Chump says that this business class is the shit one, that from Calgary
Or Toronto or Vancouver they'd be in lay-flat pods. But she puts
The noise cancellation on her headphones and thinks of blue
Water, cliché but what the hell else does one have for dreams these
Days. And who cares what some business bro thinks? She watches
Out of the side of her pretend-sleeping eyes as he pulls up document
After document loaded with indecipherable jargon about Impact and
Forecasting, Trends, Systems Analysis and other shit that doesn't
Actually mean anything and she wonders why the hell they have to
Live in this stupid world, with their stupid made-up jobs, with their
Stupid made-up monetary system that doesn't mean anything. It's
All make-believe. And she thinks that maybe if Chump dropped fifteen
Pounds she might pay a bit more attention but he's got these chubby
Cheeks and she can't tell if he's 25 or 50 or somewhere in
Between and doesn't want to invite in a boring conversation when she's
Going to read that fucking novel, and sit on the beach with a million drinks.
Stumble back to her room after lunch and have one of those naps where
The alcohol and sun and sound of the ocean lull you into the best sleep
In years.

Aho,
Buddy is trying to figure out how to meet women
And it's not going well at all. Stoner Cousin told him to
Keep the trapline open, whatever that means, but he got
A whole bunch of matches when he first booted up Hinge
But then shit went sideways and he hasn't even so much
As struck up a conversation with anyone
Since Dene Lady went running out of his place. Just nothing
No matches, no conversations, nothing at all and he can't believe
That he paid forty fucking bucks for this dumb-ass app.
What's a guy to do? The only thing worse than being 34 and alone is
Being 35 and alone and his birthday is coming up fast and
This just isn't really how he thought things were going to
Turn out. Didn't think he'd be sitting by himself night after
Night wondering where all his old friends went, wondering
Where all the good times went, wondering when the last time
Anyone actually asked him to hang out was. Can't remember
That, he's either gotta pester a friend to hang out or he won't
Hear from them and he never thought that he'd actually be
Lonely or know what that really meant. Means. Almost starts craving
Work cause at least there he has people to talk to and go
Out for supper with, smoke a couple late-night darts and shoot
The shit. And he realizes that somehow he's become that guy
Who cares more about work than he does anything else because
That's all you have to hold back the loneliness. Thinks a lot about
The bush where they scattered his grandfather's ashes years ago
And thinks that if there was ever a good place to die it would be
Right beside him. Thinks a lot about Baby Momma and what she's doing
And if she ever thinks of him but he's too scared to send a message
Because a guy doesn't actually want to know what's going on. He
Already knows from his dreams that come every night. Hasn't slept
Since they broke up and that might be fucking him up a bit.

Aho,
Baby Momma snagged up. Not the cute prof boy that teaches
Her classes. But some guy that she met out at the Cree one
Night when her cousin had all the kids over at her house. He
Was throwing minimum bets down on the roulette table and
Smoking cigarettes and laughing with his buddy and he had
A nose that looked like it had been punched in a time or two
He smiled at Baby Momma and she thought a lot about how
She hadn't fucked anyone in a long time. And maybe this was
The night. She went to put a bet down on black and he told her
To rub his bald head. That it was good luck. Later when they
Were back in his hotel room, puffing cigarettes in sweaty makeup-
Stained sheets, she told him that an old Cree teacher told her
That bald people were considered the holiest back in the day
Because they're closer to the creator. He laughed and laughed
And said he'd worship her instead of any creator, and she forgot
That white guys can't get past the idea that every god has to be
A physical manifestation of themselves in some way. But she
Didn't mind the way he went to church with his tongue all over
Every inch of her body.

Aho,
Fancy University Boy likes smoking out back after shift
With the kitchen crew. Bunch of tatted-up, chain-smoking
Hard-drinking stereotypes from the books he read back in
The day about any kitchen ever. But they have a better vibe
Than the guys back in the warehouse who haven't sent him
A single message since he got shitcanned a couple months
Back now. And here he is with the first fucking steady thing
He's had going in a while. Not that he's going to be paying
Anything off anytime soon but he can snag a few packs of
Smokes here and there and go to the pub around the corner
To watch the one lady who preps with 780 HAF tattooed on the
Inside of her wrists absolutely destroy old 2000s songs when
Her name gets called to step up for karaoke. He likes the way
That her brown roots show when she ties up her dyed blond
Hair and how she's never said anything to him except a grunt.
Maybe tonight will be the night he thinks every time he puts the
Apron on and steps into the dish pit to greet the unending splatters
Of gravy and ketchup and caked-on cheese from too many poutines.
NDN Cook shows him the odd thing on the side, how to chop something
What to yell, how to navigate all the fucking hot shit that can burn
A guy. Thinks that he's going to get some comments, something
About a powwow, but the rest of the kitchen doesn't give a shit.
That's warehouse shit. The kitchen is more concerned with where
They're going to score a clean baggy tonight, something not cut.
Grunt girl has a naloxone kit attached to her bag and FUB wonders
If she's ever had to use it.

Aho,
Aunty Prof didn't fuck the white business bro but she did
Have a religious moment with her vibe, the one that she was so
Nervous about going off in her bag when she was going through
The airport that she made sure to take all the batteries out beforehand.
Still would call that a success because she didn't have to lay
In bed and wonder when the fuck he was going to get out
Of her room and leave her alone. Good vacation all around and
Her brown skin is popping now that she's back on campus.
At least she's got that. The pasty fucks might have the jobs
Status, tenure, course releases, sabbaticals, reduced teaching
Loads, time for research, grants, and benefits. But she looks
Fucking good and she will her entire life, just like all her aunties.
So there's that at least. Aunty Prof thinks that she should start
Looking for one of those corporate gigs, something where they
Just want a brown face on staff to say that they're living up to
The TRC, UNDRIP, D&E committee goals, whatever, get money
Get laid. She used to think that she was going to change the world
How quickly that notion gets beaten out of you as you have
To roll through what it actually means to be an adult in a Western
Capitalist culture. Even if that same culture is on your territory.
She likes to listen in to the conversations of her students who
Still have the idealism that comes with being in your late teens
And early twenties and wishes that she could muster the passion
That they have for revolution for anything. It feels like a long time
Since anything really made her feel something. Is that the same
Thing that happens to the pasty fucks that she works with? Is that
Their secret revenge on her?

Aho,
Buddy was yapping with his friend on the phone
Other night on shift. Was a long one waiting for a hotshot
Truck to show up. Killing time calling up anyone who would
Listen and he starts yapping. Talking a bit through what's been
Going on and his friend goes and suggests that he go talk to
Someone. Buddy stumbles and his friend says, "yeah
Like a therapist" and Buddy laughs into the phone. "What kind
Of white shit is that," Buddy says. His friend tells him it was
Just a suggestion but the conversation is over and Buddy's back
To smoking in his truck with the window cracked a ball hair
And wondering if it wouldn't be better if he just ran a fucking
Exhaust pipe into his truck and called it good? Better yet get in the way
Of one of the swinging rigs on site and go down so the kids
At least get a payment. But did he actually update his forms?
Would they get anything? How does that even work?
Stoner Cousin told him that he saw Baby Momma at the Cree
With some bald dude and Buddy Man wasn't sleeping before
But now he's definitely not. Feels like it's been months but every time
He falls asleep he dreams of her, and bad dreams too, where
She's hooking up with someone. Or he's going back to talk to
Her but she's just telling him what he already knows. And he
Can't believe that he has to relive all of this every single night
When he closes his eyes. Can't believe he has to go through
Every day thinking about his dreams. Wishes that the two of them
Weren't so tied together. Wishes that the two of them didn't have
That bond that makes him think that maybe it would be a lot
Better to step in front of the pipe than try to fall asleep that night.
Fuck a therapist. Buddy needs to get so fucking drunk that
He doesn't dream.

Aho,
Bald boy keeps texting Baby Momma but she's not sure
How to respond. What does it mean when you're so
Wrapped up in supporting a bunch of kids and some
Aunties and uncles who blew through the first payments
Coming out of the Nation in a long time. Doesn't want to
Add a white boy to that list, but maybe the white boy will
Actually support her. But she doesn't know how
To not think about Buddy when she's texting him back. Is
He going to be another guy who's gone all the time and only
Messaging her when it's convenient? Does she even need
That at this point? Her friends and her sister tell her that she's
Overthinking it all and that a hookup is good for her to process
And move on. Got enough to deal with the whole school
Thing and everything else going on. Adding something else into
The mix might not go well. So she leaves the texts on read and
Watches the days go by as they fade into the night. At least
A bald boy knows how to keep a close shave and not let the
Stubble scratch away for a long time.

Aho,
Line cook calls in sick and Fancy University Boy got the nod
To hop in and replace him. Only fucked up a couple times, dropped
A few things, screwed an order up, but nothing that doesn't happen
On the regular. And everyone yelled at him and got mad because of
The rhythm of it all. But at the end of the night they took Fancy University
Boy out for a couple beers at a dingy-ass pub down the way and he
Feels like he knows what he wants to do now and it doesn't involve going
Back to school in any way. Even though he gets veiled phone calls from
The Métis Education Authority and his parents telling him to smarten the
Fuck up and get back enrolled. They might even forgive his debt and give
Him some more cash to get going again. Say they don't do that for everyone
But they will make an exception for him, but Fancy University Boy knows that
It's only because like three dudes have successfully finished university in the
Past couple years and they need to get that stat up. And it's just money that
They have to blow, veiled threats, and he tells them to get fucked. He's good.
Over a smoke NDN Cook talks about a program he did at NAIT that helped him
Figure out the flow and understand what food goes with what. Fancy University
Boy says that seems unnecessary for throwing shit in a deep fryer and NDN Cook
Stares him down and tells him that he's not getting the point of it all if he's still
Thinking like that. NDN Cook tells him to give his head a shake and then blows
Cigarette smoke towards the Niskwak Highway.

Aho,
Chair comes back to Aunty Prof and tells her that her classes
Have all been switched to a different day. The little tenured shit
Decided that he needed Thursdays off for "research" and Aunty
Prof knows it's because he's doing consulting work on the side as
An expert on Indigenous futurisms. Speaks a good talk that one
And knows to bring in a couple "elders" that he has on the grant
Payroll. Aunty Prof planned on spending Thursdays with her
Friend who runs a Knowledge Keepers circle at the public library
Where they go around doing informal book clubs and very formal
Ceremonies with people at the different branches, well mainly the
Inner city and north side ones. But now that's all gone and she knew
That shit like this would happen but fuck, was just hoping for
This one work thing to get her through the next semester. Tells the
Chair about her community-based research project and the Chair
Just shrugs and says, "it is what it is." Which is exactly what her friend
Said but with a completely different tone. Aunty Prof wishes that
It wasn't always coming back to this competition vibe and that she
Could just teach the Indigenous students, and the first- and second-
Generation students who came to the lands because of colonialism
And understand what that really is because they've seen it first-hand.
Not some old school settler guilt shit. A Somali woman in her class
Tells her that she loves her territory but doesn't want to be here. She'd
Rather be back home but can't because of imperialism and colonialism
And all the shit that comes with it. And Aunty Prof starts thinking about
What it would be like if she had to leave her territory and can't imagine
What her students have gone through. Same shit. Different levels.

Aho,
Buddy Man doesn't go and see a therapist. But he did start
Googling away on if there were any "Indigenous" ones available.
There weren't. Obviously. But he did at least google it which he
Considers a start and almost booked an appointment with a
Lebanese lady because he knows that up in Lac La Biche the
Métis and Lebanese have created their own subculture through
Banging away during the long winter nights. Mohammed Gladue's going
Back to Beirut. Love Lac La Biche. The best-run A&W on goddamn Earth in
Buddy's not-so-travelled opinion. His nohkum's family lived on
A road allowance not too far south of here back in the day and he
Feels a connection to the space because of it, even though his
Family was displaced up here from Edmonton. Learned that from
His Fancy University Boy cousin whose family had all that knowledge.
Buddy spends most of his nights on days off crying away. Doesn't know
What to do with himself since he can only see the kids on the odd one
And he wishes that he figured something else out. Did he really need
To work so much? Did he really need to work out of town? Could have found
Some warehouse job in the city and made three-quarters less than what
He does but he would have at least been home. And what does
All this money and shit matter when he spends every single night alone?
Wants to know if Baby Momma is thinking about him as much as he thinks
About her which is every single fucking second of the day. He thought
It would get easier at this point, but it's been months and he's more depressed
Than he's ever been. Stopped even attempting to go out on dates a few
Months back, now he just wallows on the couch for hours on end watching
YouTube videos of stupid golf challenges and video game players, the most
Mind-numbing shit. But he can't even stomach watching a TV show if there's
Any invested romantic interests in it. Which there always are. Maybe he'll look
Back into a therapist when he gets off the next shift. Or maybe he'll just grab
The old shotgun and blow his head off.

Aho,
Baby Momma decides to go on an actual date with Bald Boy.
He kept texting, and texting, and texting and she didn't think
She was going to but then she wanted to fuck and her sister
Told her that she didn't have anything to lose. She knows he's
Not sketch because they were already alone in a hotel room
And that's usually when shit goes down. So she got that over
With and Baby Momma wasn't worried about that but now she
Is but Bald Boy asks if she wants to take his dog for a walk and
Then hit up a brewery. She tells her sister that and her sister
Says that Bald Boy is definitely a hipster and she doesn't have
Anything to worry about, at least not physically, he'll probably try
And pull some weird white settler guilt trip shit at some point but
Whatever. And Baby Momma doesn't think that she's actually gone
On a date in years and years and years. Has she ever? Not even.
So she goes and meets Bald Boy at the entrance to a park and it's surrounded
By so many people with dogs that get more love than most of the kids
In the world. Bald Boy drives a Lexus but he tries to pass it off as an
Old one but Baby Momma notices that shit right away. His dog is cute
And runs around playing and getting pets and doesn't cause any shit
And she thinks about how the old dogs that she grew up with would be
Just fucking going rank on all of the other dogs in the park right now.
Broken necks and blood everywhere. She tries to snap out of it and ask
Good questions but she can't say anything except "that's really interesting"
Anytime he brings something up. And she feels that she's acting like a
Complete fucking idiot, but he seems more than content to just continue
To talk about his job at a foundation funding education initiatives in Africa.
He's the Head of Impact or some bullshit like that and when he says it
She can tell that he expects her to be impressed. But it doesn't mean
Anything. They go for a beer and she's expecting him to invite her back
To his place. But he doesn't and just says that he'd love to see her again
And that she should text him when she gets home. She texts her sister instead
He even asked about the kids. Big butterfly lady.

Aho,
Back at his parents' for the holidays and he's hiding his new bird tattoo
And the fact that he brought a pack of cigarettes with him, trying to
Sneak one or two at night while he's going through the NAIT website
And it's a lot more chill than when Fancy University Boy went through
The university one. His mom convinced that he's going back to finish up
That education degree and then move back on up to the town to marry
A good Métis girl, maybe a nurse, and then start stacking up the grandkids
For her. Fancy University Boy wishes that his parents would start cooking with
Salt but his dad has some old '90s-era health fads in his head and high
Cholesterol will be the death of them all. He used to never care about the food
Thought it was all good but now he just knows that there's more to it than
Just throwing vegetables and a rough grouse or a moose roast in a can of
Mushroom gravy and boiling the shit out of it until the meat is so tough you
Gotta really rip it with your teeth to get a chunk off. Just giving er doggy style.
Trying to figure out if Métis Education will pay for the chef program but their
Website is pretty strict saying that it's just straight-up university programs.
Hoping that he can somehow sneak it in, because he knows his parents don't
Have any money and he's already gotta pay back those years of tuition and
Living expenses from his first go-around. That plus the tuition and you don't
Make shit as a cook ... but fuck it. Doesn't think he's gonna be telling his mom
That he smokes now and he's a badass line cook with a tattoo who doesn't have
To worry about how he pronounces words and if the profs like him and how
The other students in class think he's a complete dumbass and he doesn't have
To wear those stupid collared shirts or the stupid warehouse uniforms and
It's just black jeans and black T-shirts and black aprons and that's all a Fancy
University Boy needs.

Aho,
Aunty Prof spends the holidays drinking fancy wine that she can't
Really afford but fuck it. Pet-Nats and all that hipster crap that the
Local queer bookstore promotes through some side hustle game.
She can deal with that and thinks about what it would be like if she
Had a family and kids and all the other things that most people her
Age do and she thinks that it would probably be pretty nice. But here
She is, alone again, drinking wine and watching the most boring YouTube
Videos to kill time. So many daily-routine ones and she's hoping that
One of the videos will give her some sort of feeling. Aunty Prof drinks
Too much the one night and instead of getting her syllabi ready for the
Next semester like she said she was going to do she loads up Hinge
And creates a perfectly curated profile with all the good photos from the
Past year, her beside the pool with her primed workout body looking great
Her speaking at a conference, her with her granny, a couple selfies for
Good measure and one with her best friend who doesn't live anywhere close
To her anymore. That one might be a little old but fuck it. Crafts some great
Prompting questions. Honestly has more fun building out the profile than
The game that comes next when the dopamine hits come flying in with
Quick little matches and just a flood, an absolute flood, of shitty dudes liking
Her photos, the bikini one in particular. Aunty Prof wonders if anyone is
Somewhat articulate and worries that her students might see her profile.
But then again it's 2025 and who gives a fuck about that kind of thing anymore.
Definitely not the younger generation. Drinks more wine and looks at more
Profiles of electricians, and plumbers, and construction bros, realtors, a couple
Lawyers, and can't imagine ever sitting across from them and having a
Conversation. Maybe she should just get a fucking dog instead or finish that
Book of poetry that she keeps whittling away at. But someone to talk to would
Be nice. Someone to talk to would be nice. She never does finish the syllabi.

PART FOUR

CHOKECHERRIES

Aho,

Buddy's got the kids for two weeks. That hasn't happened in
The past year since him and Baby Momma split up. His mom is
Coming into town to help him out cause Stoner Cousin is useless
And Buddy's worried that he's going to be overwhelmed. Has only
Seen the kids on the odd weekend here and there and worries that
They'll run roughshod angry moose style over him. Not if Granny's
Here to kick some ass though. He's trying not to think about the fact
That the reason he's got the kids is because Baby Momma's headed
To Mexico with her new boyfriend, some bald-ass loser. Trying really
Hard not to think about it. But of course that doesn't work. He loads up
A bunch of parenting videos and goes through them. Gonna impress her
By knowing what the fuck he's doing. Can't watch anything else because
It all brings up too many feelings. Kids come flying in the door and he
Got his mom to bring down all his old Legos from the basement and the
Older kids, Peyak and Niso, just start going ham on them. Newo throws
A piece in her mouth and Buddy tries to say something to Baby Momma
But she's unloading everything on his mom and won't even look his way.
He was hoping that he might have a chance to talk with her. Actually tell
Her about the way he feels and all his regrets and how he wishes he had
Done things differently and how if she gives him another chance he'll make
Sure that it won't turn out the way it did and she must still care about him a
Bit but she won't look at him. Won't look at him. And she's off running into
The 4Runner that he paid for and gone before he gets a chance to say anything.
Which throws his entire fucking plan out the window because he thought
That maybe if they were able to talk it out that she'd fall back in love with him.
He goes on the back deck for a smoke while his mom gets the kids all sorted
And cries while he sucks it down. Wipes his tears up, goes inside, washes his
Hands, and sits down with the kids and wishes that they were all sitting down
Together like they used to.

Aho,
Who goes to a fancy beach resort with her nice bald boyfriend?
Baby Momma does, without her kids too for a few days and she's
Nervous that they'll be with Buddy but knows that his mom will have
Everything under control and she can just sit back and enjoy the sun
A few drinks, some fucking, and let her brown skin get super crispy
Before heading back to the dry-ass pale Prairies. Bald Boyfriend was
Shocked when she told him that she had never been on a plane before
Didn't understand how someone could live that type of life. And often she
Feels like she has to explain a lot of shit that he should just get. Doesn't
Understand the sheltered, isolated world that a person like him comes from.
Doesn't understand how someone could know absolutely nothing about
NDN people on the Prairies outside of some bullshit stereotypical shit that
He probably picked up in Cultural Awareness 101 at work. Baby Momma
Ignores his sometimes really dumb and probably racist inquiries and questions
And teaches him a few things here and there and often thinks about just giving
Him completely wrong information so that he might recite it and look like a
Total dork. But she doesn't because he has kind eyes and pays for a trip like this,
"All on points baby," he said. And she doesn't know what that means, nor does
She care. A lady like her deserves a vacation and a break once in a while. So
Why does she feel so uptight and nervous, like she can't shake the feeling that
She shouldn't be here. Bald Boyfriend tries to reassure her that it's all good but
She can't help pushing him away every time they sit down, can't speak as well
As she wants to, starts getting nervous around all the skinny white ladies with
Booties sitting by the pool while her non-existent Métis butt can barely fill out
The one-piece. Starts getting more nervous and more nervous as the days go by
And decides at one point that she's not sure if this life is for her. Bald Boyfriend
Says it just takes some getting used to, that's all. That's it.

Aho,

Fancy University Boy moved up to salads on the regular and he's loving
Life on the line. Likes to stare at the grill and dream about the day
That he might be in charge of ripping up steaks and burgers on that unit.
Or maybe even doing the plating and calling out the orders, making sure that
Everything is good before they throw it through the slot to the front of house
And let them take it from there. One of the servers has this smile that Fancy
University Boy can't get out of his head, and he knows it's cliché to fall in love
With every single lady that works in the pub, but hell who else does he engage
With on the regular. And whenever they catch eyes, she seems to smile a little
More than she always does, or at least he likes to think so, apparently the next
Week there's an annual New Year's party and everyone usually goes out
Afterwards. Not just the kitchen crew who Fancy University Boy spends every
Night with at this point. His mom told him that he should quit this kitchen
Thing and get a job with his cousin Buddy and start making real black gold to
Pay back his loans and get his head on straight. "Good thing about a job like
That too is you can do camp so that you can move back here," she said to him.
And Fancy University Boy left a day early, claiming that's when his ride was
Going, but really he just didn't want to hear it anymore. Only camp job he
Would do would be to cook it up but if he's learned one thing it's that he doesn't
Want to work in a Sysco-sponsored kitchen. Thinks about how the guidance
Counsellor back at his high school never mentioned just how fun it was to
Smash out salads. Always talked a big community ReSpOnSiBiliTy game.
But sometimes a guy's gotta just do what's best for him.

Aho,
Delete app, reload it, make profile, match, small talk, delete app.
Just a constant cycle that Aunty Prof finds herself in and every
Single time she starts talking to someone she can't believe
How mundane the conversation is. Is this seriously what dating
Is supposed to be like in your thirties? She wishes that she was
Back in her early/mid-twenties when there were tons of parties
That had single people at them. At least that's how she remembers
Them. But now most of her friends have kids or have moved or
Faded out into a more chill existence. And all she wants is the chance
To connect with someone. Wonders if the prioritization of work and
Studying was really worth the loneliness that came with it. She used
To feel that she got enough connection from the students and then
The pandemic hit and that sense of community just collapsed with it.
Thought that maybe she'd meet someone with a similar lifestyle
Career path, bullshit like that but it never emerged and now she just
Sits … there … all day … every day. What do people do with all
Their time? How do they get through a day? She used to find pleasure
In reading, or writing, or walking, and now everything just seems
Depressing and she can't help but wonder if this is really what life is
Going to be like from here on out. Semester starts up and she's got
Less of a course load so not as much time to really keep herself
Busy and she knows that the tenure idea is long gone so she doesn't
Really try and pursue that angle anymore. Tries to stay away from
All the little committees and shit that they try and recruit her to for her
DiVeRsE voice.

Aho,
Buddy boy has a plan. When Baby Momma comes back
He's going to talk with her and tell her about how the past
Year has been the worst year of his life and that he needs
Her back. He's going to tell her all about how he's changed
And he's got his shit in order, which he doesn't, but he knows
That he can't do anything without her in his life. So he's thinking
If he'll tell her about how he knows to prioritize relationships and
That work doesn't mean anything if he's not with her and the kids.
Buddy's going to get a job in the city and be able to be with her
All the time to support and help out, and he's going to tell her that.
This time will be different, he knows that without her he's got nothing
And he's really hoping that she might feel the same way. That she
Might also want him back and they can make it work. Whatever she
Wants he'll do if it means being with her. They have so much history.
He's hoping that she knows that and will listen to him when he tells her
About his dreams, and his hopes for them for the future, how much
She truly means to him. Really hoping that there's something there and
Even if she's with her new boyfriend that it won't matter and she knows
That at the end of the day the two of them are truly connected and
Their love can prevail over all. Buddy doesn't have anything else. He's
Been thinking about it for a long time now and even wrote down all the
Points that he wants to talk about when they meet up and chat. He texts
Her pictures of the kids playing and waits for responses. Just constantly
Looking at his phone hoping that a message from her is coming in and
That she'll say she misses him and it kickstarts getting back together. Hopes
The pictures of the kids will trigger a conversation and that she'll realize
How much she truly misses him. Buddy's got a plan. Last-resort options
And if it fails he doesn't really know what the fuck he's going to do. Tries
To write shit out while the kids are going wild dog all over the house. And
He loves having them around. Spends nights just sitting in the rooms watching
Them as they sleep and wishes that he was able to do that every night. That
Afterwards him and Baby Momma would curl up, play a game, watch
A show. Do anything together. Do everything together.

Aho,
Baby Momma's not sure what she's going to do
Feels like Bald Boyfriend didn't really appreciate the
Fact that she was stressing out about the kids, school
Life, everything and couldn't really relax when they were
On the beach. Just didn't get why she wouldn't stop
Talking about them. And she feels that he's going to dump
Her and go back to dating white women who feel like they
Belong everywhere, like the whole world was created to
Make them feel comfortable or something like that. And
Then Buddy asked if they could have a talk, and even
Though she doesn't want that, she figures it might
As well happen since they do have all the kids together
And she's worried that it's going to be something about
Him not being able to pay all the child support money
Anymore which will really fuck with her since she's got
All that tuition money that's due soon and if
She needs that to support the kids then hell well it's game
Over for the school dream. Trying to create an example for
Peyak, Niso, Newo, and Nisto about how to break through
These fucking cycles, and to show them that if she's strong
Enough to go through all of this, support them, get an education
That those kids can do anything.

Aho,
Fancy University Boy's got a girlfriend. Or at least a girl
That he's hanging out with and he's not just pretending either
To talk smack to some of the friends back home when they're
Gaming. That beautiful lady who serves on Tuesdays and Thursdays
And I mean she might not really be his girlfriend but they have
Been hanging out a hell of a lot. And holy fuck, sex is as great as
They say it is. Didn't want to tell her that it was his first time, so he
Didn't. But she figured that out real quick anyways and bugged him
For a little bit, which he loved, because where he comes from if someone's
Teasing you that means they like you. If they don't say anything or joke
At all, then you got a real problem. But he made it up, or at least tried to
By going at it over and over and over again for the entire night until she
Got in the car and drove back to the house she lives in with her sister to
Get changed for work the next day, Fancy University Boy watching her drive
Away while he smokes a dart and feels like the fucking man. He's thinking
About asking her out all proper since all they've been doing so far is just
Hooking up after her shift is over and she comes by his place. They've had
That going on for a few weeks now and he's pretty convinced that they'll
Become forever. And the next time she comes over and they're laying
In bed and he can't stop touching her he asks her if she wants to go
Grab supper with him sometime, the pasta deal on Sunday down the Avenue
Maybe. And she looks at him and says that they've got a good thing going
Right now and why mess it up by bringing in something else. He agrees and
Then later that night after she leaves and he's smoking and his roommate comes
Home all liquored up he tells roommate what she said. Roommate tells him,
"Yeah classic server shit, they don't want to actually be seen in public with
Kitchen grubs like us. Will fuck but they won't ever go beyond that."

Aho,
Aunty Prof got asked by some badass Métis women out of
Winnipeg to come and help organize/host a conference, outside
Of the confines of the Western post-secondaries. Just a Métis
Thought leadership collective bringing together people from
Across the motherland to talk about what a good future actually
Looks like. She's fired up, hasn't felt this excited about anything
In a long time, maybe the Mexico trip, but a different kind of excited,
And the ladies that asked her to come help out are certified badasses
Constantly holding the provincial associations accountable. Constantly
Holding up community in a way outside of the bullshit of a capitalist
Society that's decimated the Prairies. Aunty Prof can deal with another
Semester of whiny-ass white kids and other professors if she can get
To May, when the Red River runs free and she can walk the streets
Of history through one of god's favourite cities, Winnipeg. The badass Métis
Women told her that they've always admired the work that she does on
Modern Métis poetics, and she thought, *how the hell does anyone know what
I actually do?* But there's a few academics in the mix so someone probably
Read a paper at some point. Either way she's excited to see who's going
To go to the conference and what collective action may come from it.
She starts preparing hosting notes, going to the meetings, chatting with the
Ladies on who would be best to be there. And she's constantly envious of
How these badass Métis ladies all seem to have some cool connections
All throughout the territories. Aunty Prof is going to interview one of the OG
Métis poets for the keynote. The poet doesn't want to just stand up there and
Give a talk. Would rather it be an informal yet miked-up conversation with
Someone who understands the work and won't ask those bullshit mooniyaw-
Type questions. Aunty Prof can definitely do that. Is so nervous to share
The same stage with one of the Métis poets who essentially built up a
Collective identity for everyone under the face of intense discrimination and
Assimilation. Aunty Prof is ready.

Aho,
Buddy's got his letter. All the things that he wants to say to
Baby Momma. A list of things he regrets and wishes he did
Differently. A list of things he misses about the two of them
Together. A list of things that he feels focus a bit too much
On himself and not enough on her. But he's not sure how to
Really switch that. Baby Momma said that he could come over
And they could talk. Even though he sees her here and there
When he's picking up or dropping off the kids he hasn't actually
Said anything of substance to her since they split. Just going through
The small talk around what the kids need, how they're acting
All those things. Nothing where he actually talks about
Feelings. Which is a hard fucking thing for Buddy to do. He
Doesn't think that he's ever thought about talking them out and
It's probably why he's in the place he is. Why they broke up. If
He could have just talked, things might have played out differently.
But he didn't. But he's going to now. And he walks through the door
And the kids are off playing video games upstairs and the youngest
Newo, is sleeping and Baby Momma is sitting on a couch and the house
Is as destroyed as a house always is when there are four kids bringing
Hell on it. And she looks incredible and Buddy is so nervous that he can
Barely get the words out that he wants to say. But he does and he sits down
And he's holding his head in his hands and she's staring at him, but not
Really looking in that old Métis way. He moves his hands away from his face
To try and pronounce eloquently his words of love, and missing her, and what
A future could be for the two of them. He talks and talks and talks and she
Doesn't say much. But when she does he can see the pain in her eyes and
It didn't really occur to him how much he actually hurt her through his actions.
Buddy sits there and feels how angry and hurt she is and all he wants to do
Is hold her but she feels so far off from him.

Aho,
Baby Momma sits there and listens to Buddy talk and she
Can't help but feel that he seems pathetic. He's beautiful in
His patheticness but it doesn't resonate anymore. She appreciates
That he's trying so hard but the more he talks the more she
Realizes that it just isn't it anymore. That they don't have the
Future that Buddy talks about. It died out a long time ago now.
She tells him that, and he doesn't want to hear it, but it's the truth.
And she knows that eventually he'll get it through his thick skull
That they're not going to get back together. That moose laid down
In the bush a long time ago. Baby Momma gives Buddy a hug as
They wrap up talking and he goes and kisses the kids and says
Goodbye and she walks him out to the door. She can't help but feel
A little bad because it could be so easy, but it's not the right move.
She doesn't tell him that Bald Boy broke up with her, his Indigenous
Fetish gone when the reality of what that really meant set in. Her
Sister told her that a vacation is always a make-or-break time. And
She doesn't really care, honestly. He was pretty boring anyways.
But she knows that she shouldn't be picky about those kinds of things
Anymore. Not young anymore. She watches as Buddy drives away
And for a brief second she thinks about calling him back and them
Getting back together and things going back to the way it was. But
The way it was scares her too much.

Aho,
Fancy University Boy likes to spend most of his days rolling
Around in bed with Server Babe. She likes to tell him about
The way that her dad said he wasn't going to pay for a master's
In English after her dumb undergrad degree in creative writing.
She thinks he'll come around to it eventually once he gets sick
Of paying her rent while she figures out her life while serving.
And Fancy University Boy can't comprehend the world that she
Comes from where rent and tuition and everything else is just
Paid for by some figurehead that still wants a semblance of control
Over all things in her life. Fancy University Boy wonders if he's
Ever going to meet this guy. But he already knows the answer to
That even if he doesn't want to, since they've never hung out
Outside of his apartment and when he suggested going to her place
She said that if her sister saw them she'd lose her shit and tell her
Dad and that everything would go to hell then. Fancy University Boy
Is more than happy to do anything she wants since at the end of the
Day he still can't believe that she's laying naked in bed next to him.
So he'll roll with it all as he's always done. But he does hope that this
Can last a bit longer. Things seem to be going really well. He loves his
Job and his roommate and smoking and hanging out, not worrying about
How he's going to fit in in the classroom or the constant anxiety and dread
About assignments and tests and not belonging. Not every Métis kid
Needs a sad story.

Aho,
Aunty Prof is feeling all sorts of good. Upcoming conference
Her classes are decent this semester. She's ignoring all the
Other bullshit and doing a pretty good job of it too. It's cold as
All hell outside and she likes the solitude of walking through
The same ravines that her granny and her granny before her
Walked through. All those generations of matriarchs walking
On the same lands. And she goes to Winnipeg and the conference
Is everything that she could ever dream of. The collective action
Of the badass Métis women towards forming a community response
To all the ongoing bullshit of internal politics, government approaches
And academic distortion is exactly what she hoped for. Sometimes
It's just nice to know that you're not alone with the shit you're going
Through too. She carries that energy and tries to hold on to it by
Continuing to talk and plan with the other women around what the
Next gathering will look like. Aunty Prof is feeling only good
Energy these days. Carrying that over from the love of community.

Aho,
Buddy is going to give this dating app thing another try.
His talk with Baby Momma went about as he expected it to go but
It didn't result in the way that he wanted it to. He figures that he
Has to live with that and that maybe it is time to try again, he's been
Feeling okay. Not great. Not bad. Okay. Not thinking about putting the old
Shotgun in his mouth anymore. He realized that no matter what he
Doesn't want to place that on his kids. Knew too many people who
Went through that same shit when he was younger and saw how it
Fucked them up. Would rather at least give the kids a chance to get
By without having ol' Daddy's death hanging over their heads for life.
Buddy might be a piece of shit, but he can hold on for them. He's thinking
About trying to find a way to stay in the city. Work at one of the fabrication
Yards or plants or warehouses. Just to be a little closer and in the kids' lives.
Baby Momma told him that he can see them more often but that they're never
Going to be a thing again. He spends a bit more time on his profile this go-
Around. Gets Stoner Cousin to take some better photos of him. Takes out
The ones from five, ten years ago. Stoner Cousin says it's a good thing that
He's six foot one. "Women love that," Stoner Cousin says. And Buddy just thinks
That Stoner Cousin's an idiot. He starts going through profiles and sees a photo
Of this lady who he can't tell if she's Métis or Cree. Says she works at the uni
Teaching Indigenous literatures. Buddy doesn't know what that means but he's
Indigenous, so he sends her a message.

Aho,
Baby Momma doesn't even think about Bald Boy. She thought she
Would but then realized that he had been hanging her out
In ambiguity after their trip together. And she feels pretty fucking
Proud of herself for not having to let another man's emotions dictate
Her own. She's feeling confident, loves where her life's at even though
It's stressful, but whose isn't and if the right guy comes around then great
But she's not gonna settle for some dumbass dickwad. She did that
Before and she's not going to do it again and she's sick of guys like
Bald Boy treating her like she's the lucky one. Fuck em. They're
Lucky to date her if anything. This is going to be her
Year. The year where she nails school, continues to be a great mother
Does her part in repairing her family relationships but not going overboard
On that either, setting her own boundaries, goes to Toronto to visit her sister.
This is going to be her year. She feels a bit bad about Buddy. Wishes that
Things could have been different but she worries that it would just be back
Into the same old routine, same old rut as before. Even if they think things
Will change, and they might, there will be too much history behind them to
Really make things great again. Are they ever great again? Sure they could
Get into it for the kids, but the kids seem quite fine now. They honestly didn't
Take much adjusting at all since he was already gone for work all the time and
Now they just see him on weekends and the only difference is she's not there.
Not a big deal. That's not her life anymore. She's got things set up on her own.
Might try and make out with the prof, it might be funny to watch a white-passing
Métis boy like that squirm a bit. Guy loves to talk Land Back and she could
Show him what that actually means. All that talk about matriarchal
ReSpOnSiBiLitY.
Like he knows shit. Baby Momma though. She's living it.

Aho,
Fancy University Boy is thinking about changing his name to
Boss Ass Kitchen Dude. Which probably won't stick but he should
Really do something since he thinks that it's been a while since he
Spent any time in a classroom. He does fancy the idea of
Himself as a writer though, and spends a lot of time reading biographies
Of cooks who were also writers. Loves those kitchen stories even if
They aren't truly representative of what he's doing. Good exaggeration is
Needed and he remembers reading in a textbook once about how the Métis
Were loud and boisterous and loved building up a story with little lies to
Make it pop for an audience. He can do the same thing and he starts
Telling people that he's a writer. No one questions that. If you're a musician
Someone will inevitably ask you to play an instrument, but no one's ever
Going to ask a writer to read something. Boring. So he can roll with it and he
Will be a writer eventually just needs to actually sit down and put something
On paper. He likes to tell Server Babe that and she loves to hear it because it's
Just another thing that could potentially piss off her family. Oh a Métis writer
Who works in a kitchen is the guy you're sleeping with. Cool. They're still going
But there's another lady who just started working front of house who flirts with
Him and it's taking him a little bit to think that two women could possibly be
Interested in him at the same time. And she might not be, but she works
Different shifts and Fancy University Boy loves getting her to fill him up a glass
Of Coke Zero and then having a beer after shift while she complains about all
The dudes who try and add her to Instagram. He likes to sit there and listen
To her, and could all night, just loving the fact that he'll never have to wear a
Sweater vest again to try and fit in and he doesn't give a shit anymore about
Gonna, going to, and turning D's into T's.

Aho,
Aunty Prof is out walking through the ravine listening to the woodpeckers
Call her home and she's thinking about how she's just going to ignore
All the shit at the university and not worry about it anymore. Not her
Problem. Just be there for the students who want her to be there for them
And not force anything. Her real work is within the community structures that
She values more than anything and in supporting the continued growth of
Métis literatures and their place within the Indigenous canon. She's turning
Around a bend and thinking about a time an owl swooped her very close to
This exact spot and she had to run home and smudge. She hears a bit of a
Screech and worries that same owl is coming for her. But it's just three kids
All way too young to be out by themselves, ripping down the path towards
Her. A voice calls out from somewhere in the woods, "Peyak, astam. Slow
Down, damnit." And out comes this dude with a baby strapped to his
Back. He looks like he's straight out of the bush and she's not quite sure
What the hell he's doing right here in downtown Edmonton, seems like an
Apparition. He stops and says hi to her and she points him in the direction
Of the other kids. She can't stop smiling at him. He looks ridiculous, all sorts
Of gruff and tough but with a kid strapped to him and a gaggle running away.
Flustered guy but he laughs and doesn't quite catch her eye. And she realizes
That she recognizes him from the dating app because he sent her a message
She didn't respond to, because she's not responding to any of them. And his
Fancy clothes looked like they came from the bargain sale at Le Château which
She immediately realizes is the exact problem with online dating, instant
judgement. She wonders if he knows that. But he doesn't seem to bring it up.
So Aunty Prof volunteers to walk with him to go and find the kids, who they
can hear laughing somewhere off in the distance under woodpecker calls and
magpie cackles.

Acknowledgments

The staff at the Next Act pub during the winter months of '23–'24, where I wrote this entire book on long, lonely nights after I finished teaching.

Jordan Abel and Marilyn Dumont for the constant writing guidance. Matthew Weigel for help with the fonts and cover design. Cody for being a great agent/friend.

The crew at Arsenal Pulp for recognizing the ridiculousness of a poetic novella and working on it with me.

My dogs, family, and friends, none of whom can read, so they'll never see this.

PHOTO CREDIT: JAY WALKER

CONOR KERR is a national award-winning (and losing) Métis/Ukrainian writer and bird hunter living in amiskwaciwâskahikan (Edmonton), born in Saskatoon, and raised in Buffalo Pound Lake and Drayton Valley. He is a member of the Métis Nation of Alberta. His Ukrainian family are settlers on Treaty 4 Territory. Conor is the author of the novels *Avenue of Champions* (2021), which won the 2022 ReLit Award, was shortlisted for the 2022 Amazon Canada First Novel Award, and was longlisted for the 2022 Giller Prize, and *Prairie Edge* (2024), which was shortlisted for the 2024 Giller Prize and the 2024 Atwood Gibson Writers' Trust Fiction Prize. He is also the author of the poetry collections *An Explosion of Feathers* (2021) and *Old Gods* (2023), which was shortlisted for the 2023 Governor General's Literary Award for Poetry and named one of CBC's Best Books of 2023. *Beaver Hills Forever* is his fifth book.